WARNING

This book is very, very

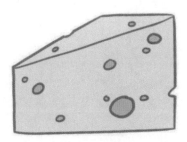

CHEESY!

I like to eat
CHEESE
in the morning

I like to put on
my big CHEESE
costume

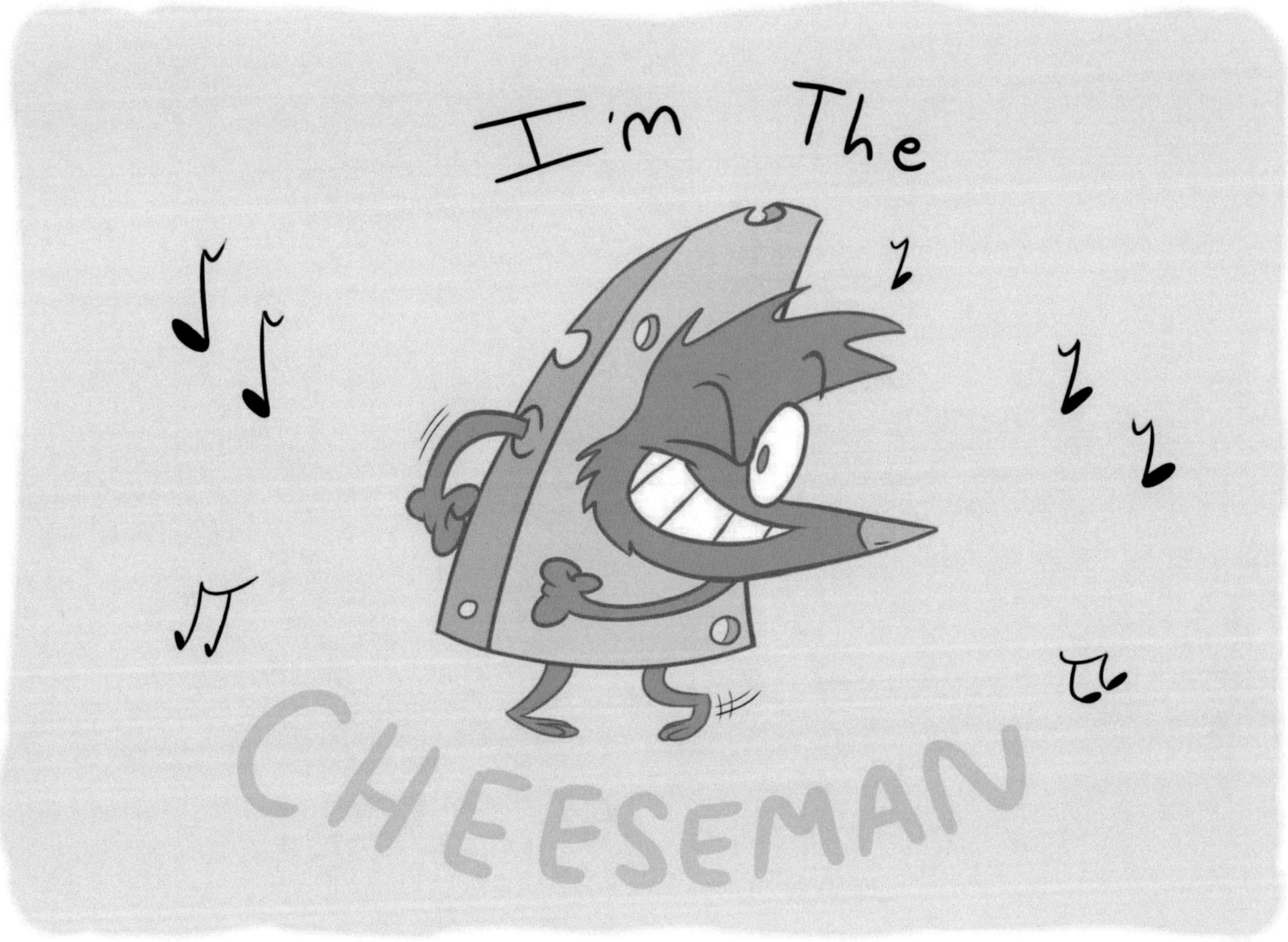
I'm The
CHEESEMAN

Bet your bottom
I Can!

I like to have
SWISS
for breakfast

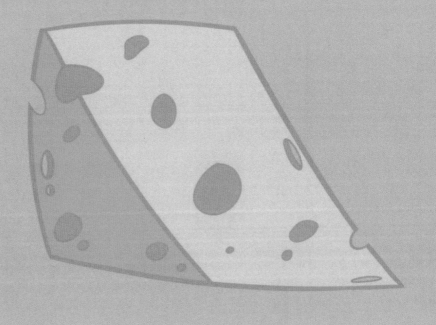

I like

MOZZARELLA

at night

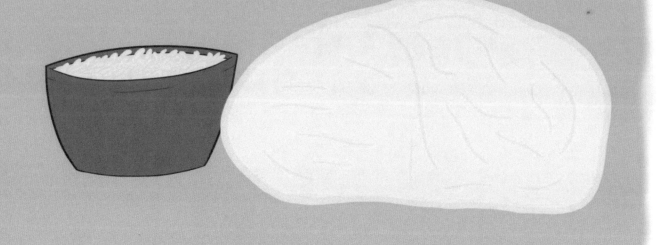

I think I'd go crazy
all through the day

I like CHEESE,
it's true

and I hope you
like it, too

And if you're going to the store

It's

CHEESE

I love it on

SPAGHETTI

I like it on

PIZZA

too

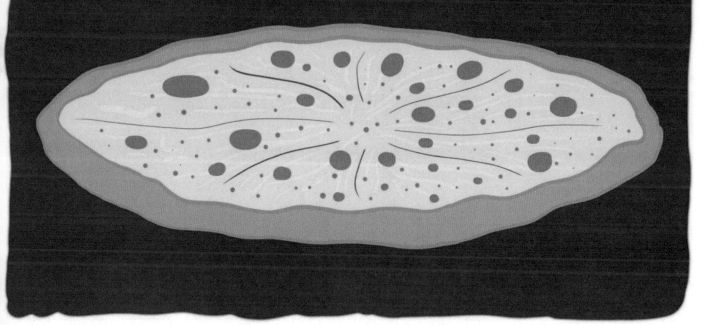

CHEESEMAN

and
Cheesewoman

Bet
your
bottom
I
Can!

I
Like
CHEESE

Made in the USA
Middletown, DE
16 October 2023

40338519R10020